THE ANGRY BIRDS MOVIE™
SEEING RED

ANGRY BIRDS MOVIE: SEEING RED
Based on the story by Sarah Stephens.
Illustrated by Tuğrul Karacan.
A CENTUM BOOK 978-1-910916-23-0
ANGRY BIRDS & ©2016 Rovio Entertainment Ltd
and Rovio Animation Ltd.
ALL RIGHTS RESERVED.
Published in Great Britain by Centum Books Ltd
Centum Books Ltd, 20 Devon Square, Newton Abbot,
Devon, TQ12 2HR, UK
books@centumbooksltd.co.uk
CENTUM BOOKS Limited Reg. No. 07641486
This edition published 2016
A CIP catalogue record for this book is available
from the British Library.
Printed in China
1 3 5 7 9 10 8 6 4 2

THE ANGRY BIRDS MOVIE
SEEING RED

centum

IT WAS A BEAUTIFUL DAY on Bird Island: the breeze was blowing, the sun was shining and the sky was very blue.

It was the kind of day that got a bird chirping, unless that bird was Red, who always started the day angry.

Red loved the hut he'd built on the quiet beach.
He had big plans to make it even better.

So when a flock of builders started drilling
outside his nest and woke him up, he fumed.

He went outside to complain,
but the bird delivering the
newspaper hit him in
the head.

Red was so mad,
he forgot about
breakfast.

TATATA

Red headed into town for a meeting.
First, he stopped at Bird on a Wire Café.
He needed to adjust
his attitude.

A snack would help. But the coffee was cold, the seedcake was stale, and the chatty waiter got on his last nerves. Red stormed off.

To make sure he was looking super sharp for his meeting, Red stopped by the hairdressers to get his wings clipped.

His hairdresser, a fancy blue canary, was doing a fine job...of annoying Red.

The hairdresser was singing really loudly and was so out of tune that Red stormed out of the preening parlour.

Arriving at his appointment, Red met with Prudence. Her job was to help birds find work. She and Red met regularly. His bad temper caused him to be fired . . . a lot.

Deep down, Prudence knew Red was a good egg and she was determined to find the right job for him.

She told him about a new job. He could start the next day. "Just try not to fly off the handle this time," Prudence said.

The next morning Red arrived at Early Bird Worms. They sold the plumpest, tastiest worms and were always busy. Red helped fill the takeout orders. He rushed to count the wriggly worms, but could not keep up with the steady stream of customers.

"Step on it!" his boss bellowed.

Red dropped the order he was filling and did exactly what his boss told him to do.

"You're fired," she shouted.

Red stomped straight over to Prudence's office. Early Worms was not the place for him and it had put him in the worst mood EVER!

But he still needed a job.

When Red entered Prudence's office again, she couldn't believe her eyes. Still, Prudence would not give up. She found Red a job at Late Riser's Worm Stand.

It was the same work as the job at Early Bird's, but less hectic. Red needed to relax.

The next morning Red slept in.
But when his alarm clock rang
he still woke up crabbier than ever.

He hated starting new jobs and two
new jobs in two days was too many.

He grumbled all the way to work.

Red arrived at the Late Riser Worms stand ready to work. But the boss was asleep and there were no customers — which was a good thing, since there were no worms to sell!

The delivery bird explained, "It doesn't matter. The shop next door, Early Bird, always gets the worms."

Except it mattered to Red. He wanted to work. He needed money to finish his hut.

Red's squawking woke the boss, just in time for Red to quit.

Prudence was amazed that she was seeing Red so soon! Here he was stomping into her office – again!

This bird is crazy as a loon, she thought. His file was nearly as tall as she was!

Finding him a job that he could keep was making *her* job impossible.

"What happened this time?" she asked.
Red was too mad to speak. "Never mind.
I can guess."

Prudence persevered. She found a job for Red at the Nap Bar, one of the most relaxing places on Bird Island.

The next morning Red learned how to load birds into rest-nests.

Once the nests were full, Red could nap too. Sleeping on the job sounded like a dream. Plus, Red couldn't get mad if he was asleep.

Red filled the nests with drowsy birds, and then climbed into his own rest-nest and drifted off to sleep, but he wasn't asleep for long.

HHOONNGKKKSHU... HHONNGKSH...

What was that awful noise?

Red discovered the source. The napping birds were snoring!

Red shook and shushed the noisy snorers, but as soon as one bird quieted down, another started making a racket.

"This isn't a dream job, it's a nightmare!" he yelled.

The birds woke up angry – just like Red, who was promptly fired.

This time Prudence was done
and so was her job list.

"I'll take anything!" Red pleaded.

Prudence remembered one last job: a job
everyone hated. "You have to deliver cakes
to bird-day parties and entertain the guests
and wear a costume," she said.

As long as he could fix up
his hut, Red didn't care. He
started immediately.

Red looked funny in the crazy getup. He looked so funny that he almost laughed himself!

"This might just be my best job yet! What could possibly go wrong?" Red said.

Prudence had to agree, but she was laughing too hard to speak.